Dear Parent:
Your child's love of reading starts here!

Every child learns to read in a different way and at his or her own speed. Some go back and forth between reading levels and read favorite books again and again. Others read through each level in order. You can help your young reader improve and become more confident by encouraging his or her own interests and abilities. From books your child reads with you to the first books he or she reads alone, there are I Can Read Books for every stage of reading:

SHARED READING
Basic language, word repetition, and whimsical illustrations, ideal for sharing with your emergent reader

BEGINNING READING
Short sentences, familiar words, and simple concepts for children eager to read on their own

READING WITH HELP
Engaging stories, longer sentences, and language play for developing readers

READING ALONE
Complex plots, challenging vocabulary, and high-interest topics for the independent reader

ADVANCED READING
Short paragraphs, chapters, and exciting themes for the perfect bridge to chapter books

I Can Read Books have introduced children to the joy of reading since 1957. Featuring award-winning authors and illustrators and a fabulous cast of beloved characters, I Can Read Books set the standard for beginning readers.

A lifetime of discovery begins with the magical words **"I Can Read!"**

*Visit www.icanread.com for information
on enriching your child's reading experience.*

HarperCollins®, 🐾®, and I Can Read Book® are trademarks of HarperCollins Publishers.

Land Before Time: Cera's Shiny Stone © 2007 Universal Studios Licensing LLLP. The Land Before Time and related characters are trademarks and copyrights of Universal Studios and U-Drive Productions, Inc. Licensed by Universal Studios Licensing LLLP. All rights reserved. Printed in the United States of America. No part of this book may be used or reproduced in any manner whatsoever without written permission except in the case of brief quotations embodied in critical articles and reviews. For information address HarperCollins Children's Books, a division of HarperCollins Publishers, 1350 Avenue of the Americas, New York, NY 10019. www.icanread.com

Library of Congress Catalog card number: 2007926270
ISBN 978-0-06-134777-1

Typography by Rick Farley   ❖   First Edition

I Can Read!

Cera's Shiny Stone

Adapted by Catherine Hapka
Based on the teleplay "Canyon of the
Shiny Stone" by John Loy
Illustrated by Charles Grosvenor and
Artful Doodlers

HarperCollins*Publishers*

Cera: A tough, headstrong young threehorn.

Tria: Cera's stepmother.

Petrie: A clumsy clown of a flier.

Littlefoot: A happy, friendly young longneck.

Tria makes a pile of stones.

She puts a shiny one right on top.

"Pretty, isn't it?"

she asks Cera with a smile.

Cera nods.

It's the prettiest stone she ever saw!

When Tria leaves,

Cera tries to get a better look.

But the pile is too tall.

Cera tries again
to see the shiny stone.
But the whole pile tumbles down!
The shiny stone rolls away
and falls into the river.

Tria is upset when she returns.
"All you care about is
your pretty stone!" Cera cries.
She thinks Tria likes the stone
more than she likes Cera.

Cera tells her friends
about what happened.
They know it was an accident.
They think she should tell Tria
she is sorry.

But Cera has a better idea.

"I know!" she says.

"We can go to the

Canyon of Shiny Stones

and get Tria another pretty stone!"

Everyone agrees except for Petrie.

The Canyon of Shiny Stones

is near Smoking Mountain.

Petrie thinks that

Smoking Mountain is a bad place.

"It's too smoky," he says.

"And sometimes it gets all shaky!"

But he doesn't want the others

to think he is afraid.

So he finally agrees to go along.

The friends start walking.

Soon they reach Smoking Mountain.

"Not much farther now,"

Littlefoot says.

Cera thinks the mountain is pretty.

"See, Petrie?" Cera says.

"Nothing to be scared about."

"I'm not scared!" Petrie says.

And he knows how he can prove it.

He flies off over Smoking Mountain!

The others are surprised.

They watch Petrie fly.

"He's doing it!" Cera says.

"I'm doing it!" says Petrie.

Then the mountain
starts to rumble.

Rocks fly up at Petrie
and smoke billows all around him!

"Oh, no!" Petrie says.

He flaps his wings as hard as he can.

Finally he makes it back

to his friends.

The mountain stops shaking.

Petrie's friends are happy.

But Petrie is upset.

"This mountain doesn't like fliers!"

Petrie says. "I made it mad!"

"Petrie, you didn't

make the mountain mad," Cera says.

But Petrie is still worried.

"I won't fly over it ever again,"

he says.

The friends walk some more.

"Here we are," Littlefoot says.

Just ahead is

the Canyon of Shiny Stones.

Beautiful stones are everywhere.

"I don't know which one to choose!"

Cera says in amazement.

Suddenly she sees a stone

even more beautiful than the others.

But the stone bounces away.

"Somebody grab it!" she yells.

Uh-oh!

The whole canyon is rumbling.

The mountain is shaking again!

"The mountain is still mad at me!"

Petrie cries.

Cera finally grabs the pretty stone.

But Littlefoot sees red-hot lava

flowing toward them!

"We've got to get out of the canyon,"
Littlefoot yells.

The friends run as fast as they can.

Finally they spot a ledge

and scramble up to safety.

But now they're trapped by the lava!

Petrie is the only one

who can fly for help.

But he is afraid of

making the mountain even madder.

"How much madder can it get?"

Cera asks.

"Petrie, we're counting on you,"

Littlefoot says.

Petrie is very, very scared.

But he has to help his friends.

"I'll go," he says.

He flies over the mountain.

And the mountain stops rumbling!

Petrie gasps in surprise.

Maybe the mountain

isn't mad at him after all!

"Don't worry, guys!"

he calls as he flies toward home.

Petrie brings back the grown-ups.

They rescue the kids from the ledge.

"We came here to get you this

new shiny stone," Cera tells Tria.

Then Cera drops the stone!

"Oh, no!" Cera says sadly.

"I'm just glad you're safe, Cera,"
Tria says.

"You're much more important to me
than any shiny stone."

Tria smiles at Cera.

Cera smiles back at Tria.

The others get ready to walk home.

But not Petrie.

He's going to fly!